KITTY is not a CAT

Teddy's Bear

In a rundown old mansion perched on a hill there lives a family of stray cats. These cats play music, love parties and live without a care in the world.

MEET

The Nazz

Last Chance

King Tubby

Cheeta

Petal

Mr Clean

AND

Timmy Tom

One day, a small girl with two black pigtails knocks on the cats' front door. Before they know what's happened, she's moved in! The cats have a firm **NO HUMANS** policy, but the girl isn't like regular humans. She wears a bright orange costume with ears and paws and a tail, and she says

Not that the cats know what that means.

Her name is **KITTY** – they read it on her collar. It seems all Kitty wants to be is a cat. **But...**

Teddy's Bear

JESS BLACK

LOTHIAN
Children's Books

As autumn drew to an end and the weather grew cooler, Kitty and the cats found themselves spending more and more time indoors. King Tubby decided that Kitty needed a new toy to play with during the colder months ahead. A **teddy bear**, to be precise.

He tasked four of the cats with the important job of finding the perfect one.

There was only one teeny, tiny, little problem. 'I'm not sure anyone here actually knows what a teddy bear is,' The Nazz muttered to Last Chance.

Nevertheless, the next day the cats and Kitty all gathered in the library for the presentation of the teddy bear.

Kitty was fizzing with excitement. A teddy bear of her very own? She imagined what it would be like – **soft** and ever so **cuddly**.

King Tubby waved Timmy Tom over to inspect his gift first.

'I found this in a cereal box!' Timmy Tom said brightly.

He was the youngest member of the household and felt certain he knew exactly what would make the best bear for Kitty.

King Tubby puffed up his rather portly chest. 'Hmm, I believe teddies have more **fluff** and less **wheels**...'

Tubby was right. Four wheels, four doors and two headlights? It looked more like a car than a teddy to Kitty, but she didn't want to hurt Timmy Tom's feelings.

'Meow!' Kitty thanked him.

'Full points for trying, Timmy Tom,' said King Tubby. 'Next! Petal, do you have a **teddy bear** for Kitty?'

'I have lots!' Petal said breathlessly. As usual, she could hardly contain her enthusiasm. 'Oh, Kitty, dear, I hope you like these.' She held out a packet of mini biscuits in the shape of bears.

King Tubby opened the packet and helped himself to a handful, spraying crumbs everywhere.

'They *are* bears,' Tubby agreed as the crumbs fell from his mouth, 'but they are also...

all gone!'

Kitty giggled. How funny each cat's idea of a teddy bear was! She couldn't wait to see what came next.

'Mr Clean?' King Tubby asked. 'What do you have for Kitty?'

Mr Clean slowly stepped forward. He was a dirty tabby cat, so filthy that nobody – not even Kitty – knew the real colour of his fur under the layers of dirt.

'Oh, it's nothing,' Mr Clean murmured, looking at his feet. 'Just something I made.'

'You made it yourself?'

Petal said, impressed.

Petal and Kitty strained to see what Mr Clean was holding. To Kitty, it looked like it just might be a real teddy bear.

'Meow!' Kitty clapped her hands together eagerly.

'Do show us!' King Tubby agreed.

Mr Clean was just about to reveal his gift when they all heard an enormous

Kitty couldn't believe her eyes. Cheeta was standing in the doorway with a grizzly bear that was easily three times his size.

'WHAT on earth is THAT?'
asked King Tubby.

'It's a bear,' announced Cheeta. 'For Kitty!'

A real, live grizzly bear all to herself! Kitty was thrilled.

'I bought him from my friend Teddy,'
Cheeta explained, looking very pleased with
himself. 'He dabbles in grizzlies and the odd
mountain lion.'

'So... he's Teddy's bear?' King Tubby asked,
hanging back while the others gingerly
approached.

'Look at the size of his teeth!' said Timmy
Tom. 'And his claws! What if he ate Kitty?'

'He wouldn't eat Kitty!' protested Cheeta. 'This bear is completely harmless.' He patted him on the leg. 'Aren't you?' he asked the bear.

The bear **growled**.

Cheeta gave him a friendly nudge with his elbow.

The bear **grimaced**.

Then, just as Cheeta was about to tell the others **'I told you so'**, the bear sent him flying over to the other side of the room with a single punch.

The cats froze, wide-eyed.

Kitty ran straight past them all and, before the cats could stop her, wrapped her arms around the bear's ample waist.

'Oh no, Kitty!' Petal said, looking panicked. 'Be careful!'

Kitty gazed up lovingly at the bear. The bear frowned, unsure what to do. Then he bent down, picked her up and gave her face a

big sloppy lick.

That afternoon, Teddy's bear followed Kitty everywhere. Like the best kind of playmate, he was keen for any sort of adventure.

First, they tried playing dress-ups, but the bear's claws **ripped** Kitty's tutu.

Next, Kitty showed the bear how to play hula hoops, spinning the hoop on her waist. But the hoop was too small for the bear.

After that, Kitty took the bear outside
to climb trees, but even the biggest tree
couldn't hold up the enormous bear, and a
branch almost **snapped**
from right underneath them!

What else could they do together?

Just then, Kitty heard the skittering of paws on piano keys. It was The Nazz playing a favourite Bebop tune inside.

That's it: **dancing!**

It was her favourite thing to do. Kitty demonstrated her best moves, grinning from ear to ear to show the bear how much fun it was.

At first, the bear just watched her, his head tilted to one side. Then his paw began to tap in time with the beat. Suddenly he began to move, mimicking Kitty's actions.

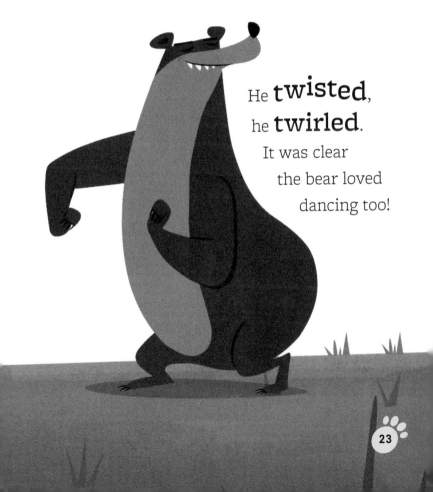

He **twisted**, he **twirled**. It was clear the bear loved dancing too!

Now, this called for a party

The cats didn't need to be asked twice.

'This is one of our best tunes yet!' Cheeta said, bouncing along to the infectious beat they were making together.

Just as the party was getting into full swing, the bear bumped into Petal mid-twirl and she landed on the floor with a thud. Kitty raced over to help Petal to her feet.

'Uh oh!' Petal gasped, looking over at the bear.

His moves had become rowdier, his arms and legs jerking about wildly.

'**Duck!**' Petal called to Mr Clean, who was playing the drums.

Mr Clean ducked just in time and narrowly missed being side-swiped. The bear's arm collided with the wall instead and his paw went straight through it.

'Oh no!' cried Mr Clean, leaping out of the way as the bear pulled his arm from the hole in the wall and spiralled back towards the drum kit.

The bear picked up
Mr Clean's drumsticks
to join in the music-making.
But he played so hard that
he bent the cymbals and
smashed all the drums
to pieces.

The rest of the cats were so focused on their instruments they hadn't noticed that the bear's enthusiasm was becoming quite a problem.

'Meow, meow, meow!' warned Kitty as the bear began dancing again.

As the rhythm sped up, so did the bear.
He spun one way and **crashed** into
the door, knocking it off its hinges.
He spun another way and
collided with a
wooden dresser,
splintering it into
matchsticks.

Then the bear turned to Cheeta, who was playing his electric guitar. The bear reached over and tried to strum along too, but he tore at the strings and broke them one by one.

'We need to do something!' said Petal, almost too afraid to watch.

'Meow, meow, MEOW!'

Kitty called to the bear, but he wouldn't slow down. He was so big and strong, what could they do?

Kitty watched helplessly as the bear danced up to Last Chance and plucked the trumpet from his hands. He gave it a huge

TOOT TOOT TOOOOOT

before squashing it flat as a pancake on the floor.

'My trumpet!' wailed Last Chance.

The bear had already moved on – he was dancing in the direction of The Nazz's keyboard. But The Nazz was too quick.

'Oh no you don't!' he said, running from the room as fast as he could, the bear right behind him.

Once the music had stopped, the bear calmed down again. King Tubby took the opportunity to call an emergency house meeting. The place looked as if it had been hit by a bomb, not a bear.

'Kitty, this teddy is **un*bear*able!'** cried the cats.

Kitty took in the destruction the bear had caused. She could see he was not a good match for her friends or the house, but she didn't want him to go.

King Tubby drew himself up to his full height and glared at Cheeta. 'After much observation I can only conclude that this is

NOT a teddy bear.'

'Hey, I only said he was *Teddy's* bear,' Cheeta retorted.

Petal sighed. 'Tubby, you never really explained what a teddy bear actually is.'

King Tubby cleared his throat noisily and changed the subject. 'You know, it took humans a long time to figure out that real bears are not ideal toys. Years and years, actually. So the fact that we clued into this in only a matter of *hours* shows just how infinitely superior we cats are compared to humans.'

The cats did not look impressed.

King Tubby continued, 'And since the bear is not a toy, **HE MUST GO!'**

'Meow!' Kitty said sadly, hugging the bear tightly.

'Tubby's right,' The Nazz said. 'It seems that if we keep the bear we'll never be able to play music again.'

There was a collective gasp.

'Never play music again?'

Last Chance repeated.

For Kitty, the idea was too terrible. As disappointed as she felt, she knew the bear couldn't stay.

'But how do we get rid of him?' asked Timmy Tom. 'He's so

b-b-b-b-big.'

'Leave it to me.' Cheeta picked up the phone. 'I'll call my friend Teddy. We'll get another bear to help us get rid of this bear.'

The Nazz considered the idea. 'Might work. But then what would we do with the second bear?'

'I can order a third?' suggested Cheeta, already dialling the number.

'No, no, Cheeta, we just need to reason with him,' Petal said gently. She turned to the bear. 'Now, listen here, bear, we've been very patient with you, but I'm afraid –'

As Petal spoke an **icy** draft blew through the house. The bear sniffed and shivered.

'Are you listening to me, dear?' Petal asked.

The bear answered with a giant

YAWN.

Then, all of a sudden, he curled up in a ball and went to sleep at her feet.

The bear slept all through the night and into the next day. Kitty wasn't sure it was a good idea to sleep for so long. When he still hadn't woken up by lunchtime, she gave the bear a small nudge. He snorted, rolled over and

just kept

sleeping.

Finally, Cheeta announced, 'That's it. I want my money back.' He punched a few numbers into his phone. 'Teddy, the bear's a dud,' he said to his friend. Then he paused. 'First day of winter, eh?' Cheeta looked up at the others. 'He's *hibernating*.'

King Tubby looked over at the calendar on the wall. 'Of course! Hibernating. I knew all along.'

Teddy explained to Cheeta that hibernating meant the bear would sleep all through winter.

So, after much deliberation and a considerable amount of **pulling**, **pushing** and **grunting**, Kitty and the cats managed to drag the bear all the way into the garden shed, where he could sleep in peace.

And just to be safe, they put a sign out the front:

Do not disturb until spring.

That evening, Kitty sat in the conservatory gazing sadly at the shed outside. Despite all the trouble he had caused, Kitty missed the bear.

Mr Clean and Petal approached.

'Go on,' Petal encouraged Mr Clean, 'show her what you've got.'

'I made you a teddy bear, Kitty,' said Mr Clean. He handed Kitty a threadbare creation roughly sewn together from random patches and old socks.

Kitty stared at the teddy bear. Then she closed her eyes and sniffed. It smelled like sweaty feet and cat fur.

'Right, well,' Mr Clean coughed, 'I always thought teddy bears are what you give someone to show you love them. And, um...'

Kitty held Mr Clean's teddy bear close. It was **soft** and ever so **cuddly** – exactly what she had hoped for. She gave Mr Clean an enormous hug. And Mr Clean hugged her back.

'Bring it in, group hug!' said Petal, wiping a tear from her eye as she wrapped her arms around them both.

Later, The Nazz went to Kitty's room to make sure she was tucked in. Kitty was curled up in her bed box clutching her new teddy bear.

'Ready for sleep then?' The Nazz asked.

Kitty purred.

'After a **mind-boggling** amount of damage to our house, you finally got the perfect teddy bear.'

Kitty nodded and hugged the teddy bear tighter.

The Nazz winked at Kitty. 'That's the way, kid. Everyone has a different idea of what perfect means to them. What you choose to love is totally up to you.' He kissed Kitty goodnight. As he left, he said, 'Though, between us, I think that teddy could definitely do with a wash.'

But for Kitty, her teddy bear was perfect
just the way it was.

COLLECT THEM ALL!

KITTY is not a CAT
Lights Out!

KITTY is not a CAT
Teddy's Bear

KITTY is not a CAT
Hired Hound

KITTY is not a CAT
Bath Time

A Lothian Children's Book
Published in Australia and New Zealand in 2020
by Hachette Australia
Level 17, 207 Kent Street, Sydney NSW 2000
www.hachettechildrens.com.au

10 9 8 7 6 5 4 3 2

A catalogue record for this
work is available from the
National Library of Australia

ISBN 978 0 7344 1977 4

Cover and internal design by Liz Seymour
Cover and internal illustrations by BES Animation
Printed and bound in Australia by McPherson's Printing Group